Heart Trouble at Hilltop

Nicholas Allan

RED FOX

A Red Fox Book

Published by Random House Children's Books
20 Vauxhall Bridge Road, London SW1V 2SA

A division of The Random House Group Ltd
London Melbourne Sydney Auckland
Johannesburg and agencies throughout the world

1 3 5 7 9 10 8 6 4 2

Printed and bound in Italy by Lego SPA

THE RANDOM HOUSE GROUP Limited Reg. No. 954009

ISBN 0 09 940455 9

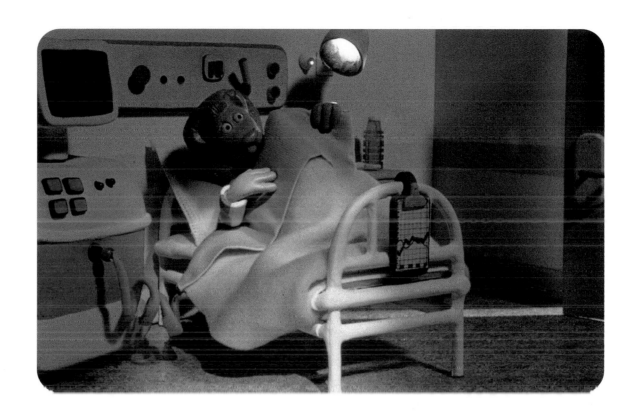

It was early morning and a very worried Dandie Lyon
lay awake listening to his heart-monitor bleep-bleeping.

'Will they ever find me a new heart?' he asked
Nurse Kitty.

'Soon, I'm sure,' she said. 'After all, it's St Valentine's
Day today.'

Kitty hurried to the staff room. She had just slipped an
envelope in Dr Matthews' letterbox when he walked in.
   'Morning, Kitty,' he said.
   'Oh, good morning, Dr Matthews! Why, look, you've
got a letter!'

Just as he was opening the envelope, the phone rang. 'Matthews here,' he barked. 'What?' He put the phone down and turned to Nurse Kitty. 'They've found a new heart for Dandie Lyon! We must tell the Teds to collect it immediately!'

They hurried off, leaving the envelope behind.

A little later, Rupert and his mum arrived at
the hospital.

'He's had these hiccups for three days now,' his
mum complained.

'Try this glass of water, Rupert,' said Kitty.

Rupert tried. 'HIC!' he went.

Meanwhile, Dr Matthews and Dr Atticus sat in the staff room munching dog-biscuits.

'Look, a Valentine card,' said Dr Atticus. 'It's for you.'

'For me? "From a Secret Admirer",' read Dr Matthews. 'It must be... Surgeon Sally!' His heart raced. 'I've been meaning to ask her out... the trouble is, I'm just not brave enough.'

'I had a Valentine card once,' said Dr Atticus. 'Oh, must be getting on eighty years now. She even left a little clue – put her name and address on the back of the envelope. I posted it by mistake.' Dr Atticus's head sunk into his shell. 'I never heard from her again.'

'Right!' Dr Matthews stood up. 'The next time I see Sally, I'm going to ask her out.'

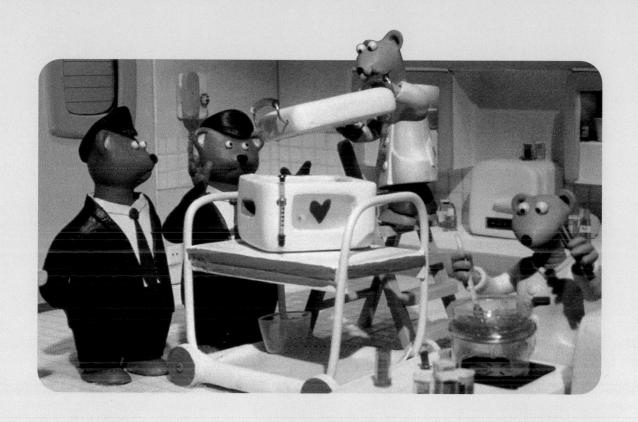

The ambulance screeched to a halt. Doors flapped. A
trolley with an ice-box on it zoomed down the corridor.

''Ere it is,' Ted said. 'Fresh as a fish.'

'Let's pop it in the fridge,' Clare, the lab mouse said.
She held up the ruby heart. 'What a beaut!'

'Careful,' the other Ted said. 'Don't want to break it,
do we? Ha ha.'

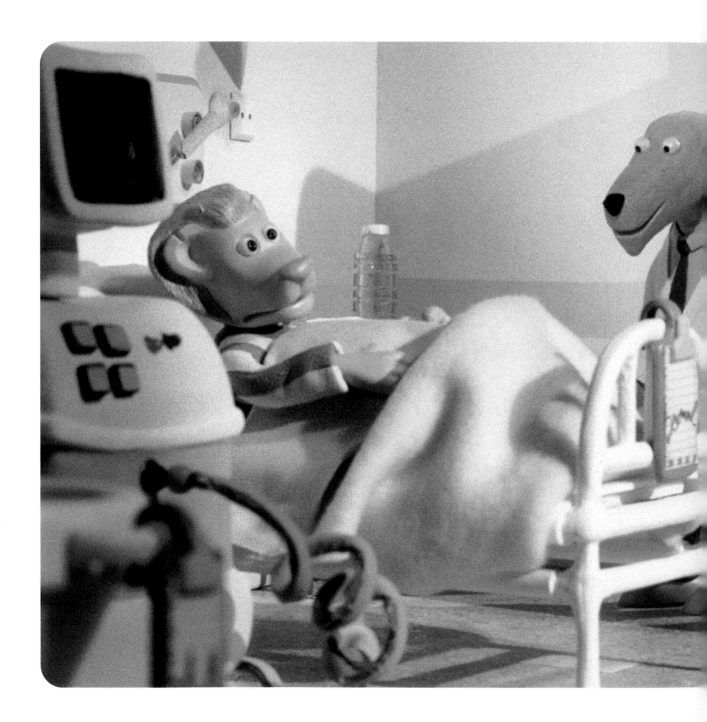

When the doctors rushed in to tell Dandie they'd found a heart, he jumped with fright.

'Oh, Dr Matthews, you know how things scare me at the moment.'

'That's why we're giving you a new heart, Dandie.'

'And we're operating this morning. So nothing to eat or drink,' ordered Dr Atticus.

It was time. The two Teds wheeled a sleeping Dandie into the operating theatre.

'Is… is Dandie definitely asleep?' asked Nurse Kitty.

'Why? You're not afraid of him, are you, Kitty?' said Dr Matthews. 'You shouldn't be afraid of Dandie. He's very friendly really. There's no need to be afraid of anyone.'

'Everyone ready!' boomed a voice.
Dr Matthews' ears stood up.
'It's you, Sally!' he said.
'Anything the matter,
Matthews?'

'N-n-n-no,' he said.
'Oh, yes there is,' said Dr
Atticus. 'Matthews has a very
important question to ask.'

'Well? Could you hurry up? I'm about to perform major heart surgery.'

'Um… um… Nothing, Sally. It's nothing.'

Dr Atticus shook his head. 'Who's afraid now, Dr Matthews?' he murmured.

Paws moved busily under the glow of the theatre lights. Voices murmured, instruments tinkled. Finally Sally ordered: 'New heart.'

'New heart,' said Kitty. The heart was removed from the fridge, then placed delicately inside the lion.

'Is it in the right place?' Kitty asked.

They listened. Suddenly the heart-monitor burst into life.

'Yes, Dandie Lyon's heart is definitely in the right place!' said Sally.

Later in the ward, an anxious Kitty peered closer into the oxygen tent. She saw Dandie's whiskers twitch. Suddenly he sat up, gnashing his teeth.

Kitty squealed.

'Good afternoon, Dandie,' Matthews said. 'How're you feeling?'

'Starving, of course, you bone-head. I haven't eaten all day!'

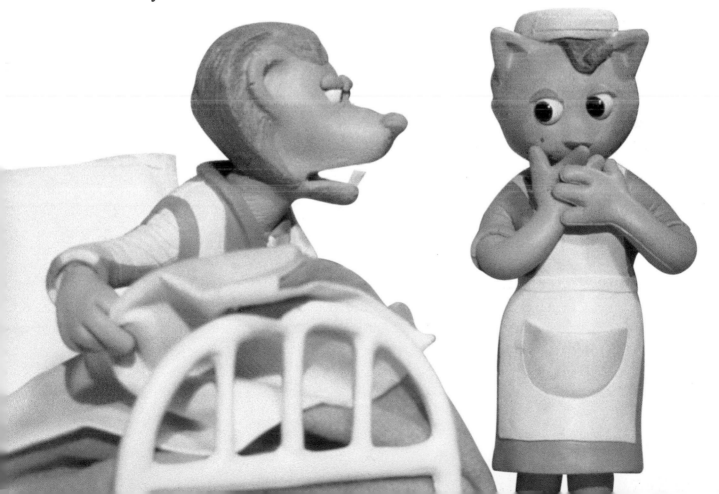

Very timidly, Kitty approached with a food tray.

'Whatcha call this then?' said Dandie.

'V-v-vegetable risotto,' Kitty answered.

'Vegetable risotto?' Dandie roared. 'You expect me to eat this? I'm going to look for some meat – right now!' Then he flung back the sheets, tipped the risotto on Dr Matthews' head, and marched down the corridor.

Dr Matthews staggered about, but when he'd finally
removed the bowl from his head, Kitty had disappeared.
He hurried into the corridor to find bins, wheelchairs,
the lab mice, and Dr Atticus, upturned.

'Where's Kitty?' he said.

No one knew. Then they heard a roar coming from
the lift. They ran to the lift doors… but the lift was
going down.

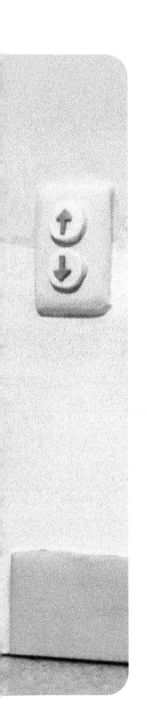

On the ground floor a little elephant was still hiccuping when the lift doors opened.

'Roooaaarrrrrr!' went Dandie.

Rupert jumped… and his hiccups vanished. 'They've stopped!' he cried. 'Oh, thank you, Dr Lyon.'

'Dr Lyon?' Dandie said, as Rupert hugged him.

'Ah, there you are, Dandie.' Kitty had arrived with a wheelchair. 'You've just had an operation!' she said. 'You really shouldn't be running around like this.'

'I'm sorry.' Dandie collapsed in the chair and started sobbing. 'I was just so hungry.'

'There, there,' Kitty purred.

On the third floor, Dr Matthews and the others
waited. When the lift doors opened, they saw Dandie,
with Rupert on his knee, sitting in the wheelchair.

Kitty pushed the chair past the astonished group.

'Well, bash me with a bone!' Dr Matthews gasped.
'Kitty was terrified of Dandie. What a nurse! What a cat!'

Dr Atticus nodded wisely. 'Well, Matthews, some are
able to conquer their fears… some, of course, can't.'

Sally was in the staff room when the door burst open.

'Oh, Matthews! You almost gave me a heart attack.'

'Talking of hearts…' Dr Matthews began. 'That was a wonderful operation you did. I thought, well, we could celebrate… Go out for dinner.'

Sally agreed. Dr Matthews was overjoyed. Then he thanked her for the Valentine card.

'Valentine card?' Sally said. 'I don't send Valentine's cards, Dr Matthews. I'm not that sort of hippopotamus. In fact, I'm not the sort who goes out to dinner either!' The door slammed behind her.

'Oh,' said Dr Matthews sadly. He began to tear up the card.

Just then Nurse Kitty came in.

'Hello, Kitty,' he said, recovering. 'You were brave going after Dandie like that.'

'He's not so bad,' she said. 'In fact, he asked me to come for dinner soon.'

'Did he?'

'Well, it *is* St Valentine's day.'

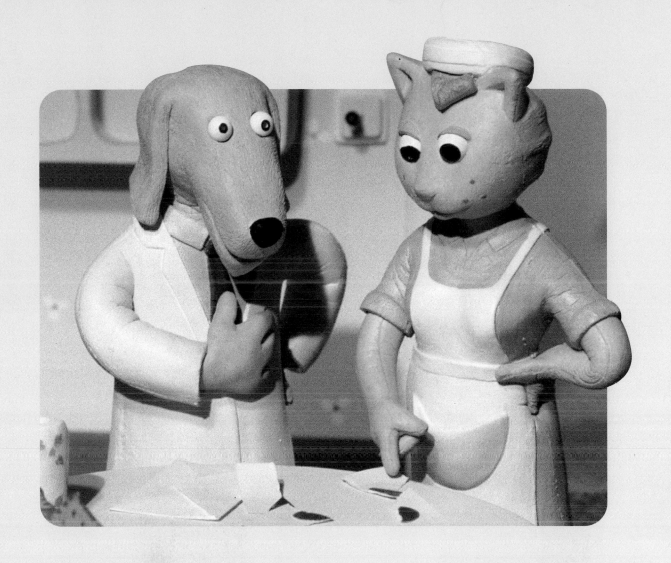

Dr Matthews looked at his torn Valentine card, and then
back at Kitty.

   'Kitty, it was you who sent the…'

   'Yes, Dr Matthews?' Kitty stepped closer.

   'Kitty… Would you… Could I invite you out to…'

   'Yes, Dr Matthews?'

The distant sound of a siren made
Dr Matthews turn to the
window. 'It's the Teds!
An emergency!
Let's go, Kitty.
We'll need a bed
immediately!'

Matthews ran out. Kitty fitted the
pieces of the Valentine card back
together, sighed deeply, then
followed Dr Matthews to the ward.